CUENTO
DE LUZ

For my little treasures Edith and Joel, so that they can discover the stories of the land where
they were born. And for their brother Gabriel, who was lucky to have been born into
a family of vanilla and chocolate.

- Marta Munté Vidal -

Kuku and Mwewe (A Swahili Folktale)

Text and illustrations © Marta Munté Vidal
This edition © 2013 Cuento de Luz SL
Calle Claveles 10 | Urb Monteclaro | Pozuelo de Alarcón | 28223 | Madrid | Spain
www.cuentodeluz.com
Original title in Spanish: Kuku na Mwewe (El águila y la gallina)
English translation by Jon Brokenbrow

ISBN: 978-84-15619-97-0

Printed by Shanghai Chenxi Printing Co., Ltd. March 2013, print number 1352-4

FSC
www.fsc.org
MIX
Paper from
responsible sources
FSC® C007923

Kuku and Mwewe

A Swahili folktale

Retold by Marta Munté Vidal

When night falls over the village of Nrao Kisangara at the foot of Mount Kilimanjaro, Deo and his brothers sit around the fire. Like every other night, they are waiting eagerly for Babu Eliamani to thrill them with a new tale.

"Hadithi! Hadithi!" whispers Babu.

"Hadithi njoo! Hadithi njoo!" shout the children.

"Open your ears and listen carefully, as tonight's tale is about to begin..."

SWAHILI DICTIONARY

KUKU hen or chicken

MWEWE eagle

KITENGE piece of brightly colored African cloth used to make dresses

MGUNGA tree in the acacia family

A long time ago, **Kuku** the hen and **Mwewe** the eagle were the best of friends.

They had been born on the same day, and felt very close to each other.

Kuku was very vain, and every year when Spring arrived,
she would go to the city to buy a **Kitenge**.

That year, she found one with the most beautiful print
she had ever seen!

She used the new Kitenge to make a dress that was so elegant that it was admired by everyone in the village.

They all stopped and stared when they saw her walking by.

"How pretty Kuku is!" and "What a beautiful dress!" they would say.

But one day, as she walked merrily across the savannah, she didn't realize that the dress had got caught on the branch of a **mgunga**, until suddenly she heard ...

RRRRIP!

Seeing that her dress was ruined, she burst into tears
and ran off to find her friend Mwewe.

The eagle didn't know what to do to cheer her up.

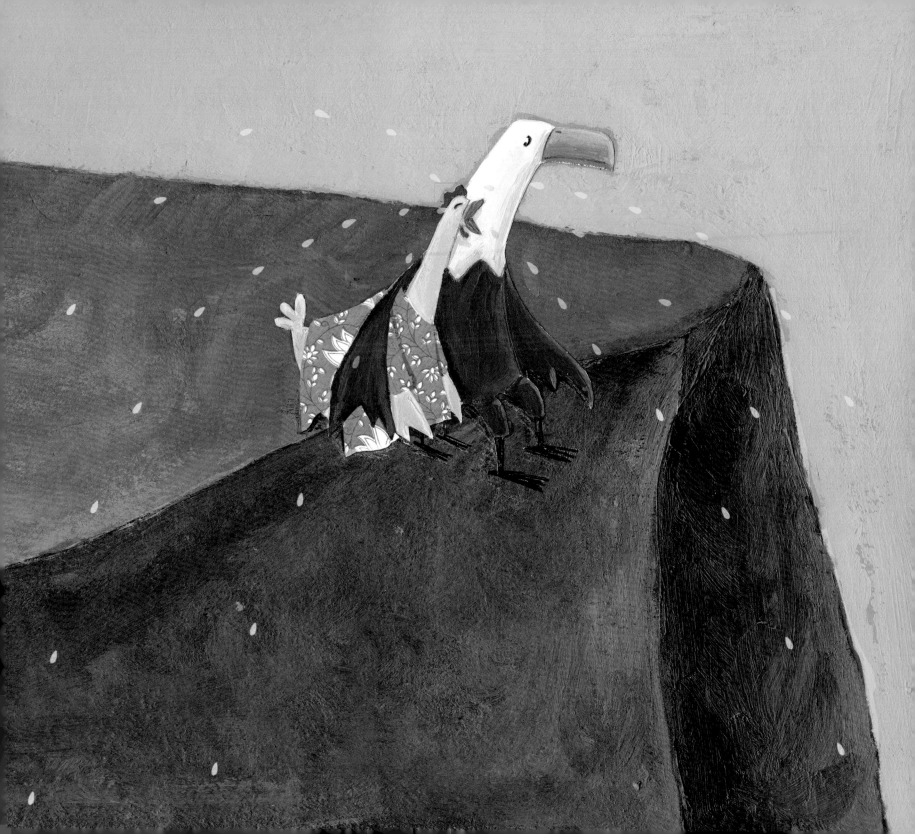

"Come into the house. I'll make you a nice cup of tea," offered Mwewe.

Kuku sat on some cushions on the floor and rested her head against the wall. Then she saw her friend's sewing needle.

It was on the shelf next to some trophies, glinting majestically on a velvet cushion like a crown!

And so, unable to argue with Kuku's logic, Mwewe reluctantly agreed to lend her the sewing needle and precious family heirloom.

"When you've finished, bring it back STRAIGHT AWAY!"

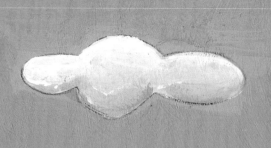

The days went by, and Mwewe didn't hear anything from Kuku about her beloved sewing needle. So she decided to fly over to the village where her friend lived to retrieve her little treasure.

But there was nobody home at the hen's house.

"Are you looking for Kuku? I saw her this morning in the market," said a neighbor from her window.

The eagle thanked Kuku's neighbor and went to the market.

The hen was very happy to see her friend.
"Hi! Look at my dress! It's as good as new! You were right; your sewing needle is more than just a needle!"
"I can see that," Mwewe replied coldly. "Could you give it back, please?"
"Of course! Oh, I thought it was here ... hang on a second, and I'll get it for you."

The days, weeks and months went by.

Despite KuKu looking everywhere, the needle was still missing.

With her wings full of presents to make up for the lost needle, the hen decided to visit her friend.

But the eagle didn't want to listen. Nothing could make up for Kuku's carelessness and the loss of Mwewe's beloved sewing needle—it was a family heirloom, after all!

"Go away, and don't even think about coming back without my treasure!" cried Mwewe.

But the needle was still lost, and so was the friendship between Mwewe and Kuku.

And from that day on, Kuku and all of the hens born since have pecked and scratched at the ground, looking for the special sewing needle that they still hope to return to the eagles.